# THE HUNTED HUNTER

Tyrone T. Berg

**WorkBook**
PRESS

WORKBOOK PRESS LLC
187 E Warm Springs Rd
Suite B285 Las Vegas NV 89119 USA

Website:        https://workbookpress.com/
Hotline:        1-888-818-4856
Email:          admin@workbookpress.com

Ordering Information:
Quantity sales. Special discounts are available on quantity purchases by corporations, associations, and others. For details, contact the publisher at the address above.

ISBN-13:        978-1-965732-19-9 (Paperback Version)
                978-1-965732-35-9 (Digital Version)


REV. DATE:      08.12.2020

# Table of Contents

# The Hunted Hunter

By Tyrone T Berg

## CHAPTER ONE

Andrew, a well dressed man about 6 ' tall man with dark hair, steps down onto the wharf from the steamer in Hobart in the early morning as the sun tries to break through the clouds.  Andrew stops, puts his bag and suitcase down and looks around the wharf area, which is nowhere near the size of the wharves along the Thames where he boarded. He notes that they are still busy with ships loading, ships unloading and a lot of people milling around, especially when a ship like the one he just arrived on is unloading it's human cargo.

He starts to look around for his likely contacts  on the wharf and spots two men one a shorter man about 5'5" with a generous sized stomach and the other a tall thin man who would even look down on Andrew so he picks up his case and bag and walks towards them.

The shorter of the two points at him and they too commence to walk over towards him the shorter of the two struggling to keep up with the fast paced taller man.  Without Andrew being able to hear what the shorter man say he notices the taller one looks around briefly with a wry smile and slows down and the shorter man catches up.  Andrew smiles at them the tall thin one nods at him in acknowledgement.

When they catch up with each other among the throng of peole Andrew introduces himself.

"Hello, I am Andrew'?

The shorter man takes Andrew's hand looking him up and down, Andrew notices this as he does so.

"Hello Andrew I am Fred Searle, it is good to finally meet you and this is Bob Rose.

Andrew turns to Bob and shakes hands with him.

"Good to meet you too Bob".

Bob replies in a friendly done with a real strong Aussie accent.

"Likewise Andrew, good trip out here I trust"?

Andrew replies with his London accent really noticeable.

"Yes, broke it up, spent time in South Africa also on zoo business. It was a great interlude to this section of this trip!  Mind you this is very different to Southern Africa!"

Bob and Fred nod agreement with Bob replying.

"Aye that it is"!

Fred indicates the direction off the wharf.

"Andrew, shall we take you to your hotel"?

"That would be good.  I am ready to go".  Andrew adds.

 Bob looks around at him.

"Is that it, two cases and a bag"? Bob asks in surprise.

"Yes I intend to buy what I require in New Norfolk which I have arranged with my contact up country in New Norfolk, Bill.  I met Bill during the war, good reliable type" Andrew explains to them.

The three of them walk towards a bright yellow car waiting for them, the driver patiently standing next to the car.  He spots them walking over and opens the  rear door and waits.

"So how was your journey on the ship out from out from London, probably not as long with the break up of it by stopping over in South Africa"? Bob asks. As he gets in the car, Andrew responds.

"Good, relaxed and I read up on your marsupials and the Tasmanian Tiger in particular and I must say a most remarkable animal.  I do look forward to seeing one in its environment and securing it for the London Zoo".

Fred gets in next.

"So you have had contact with Bill then"?

Fred makes himself comfortable as Bob gets in.

"Yes I had a telegram sent to him once my ship was underway and I sent another from Capetown as I came around the bottom of Africa".

"Not by the Suez then Andrew"? Bob queries.

"No, thought of that but in the end I thought the time spent in Africa for the Zoo was more fruitful and it was really" Andrew replies with a smile.

Fred and Bob nod agreement as the car takes off and the wharves vanish behind them.

# CHAPTER TWO

It's a dark night with the moon drifting in and out from behind the stars. Each time it emerges, it highlights the sheep grazing in the paddock. The only noise is the crickets and the odd sound of an owl hooting through the night air. The sudden flapping of bats wings as they fly low over the sheep, spooks the entire herd and they run in fright with no real directional focus.

They quickly settle down to eating the grasses around them again, as the moon momentarily vanishes and then re-emerges again.

In the tree line the sheep are being watched by a pack of three large dogs waiting for the right moment to attack. The sheep are now moving slowly in their direction, the closest of them not far from the tree line themselves. The three dogs wait, the dog either side of the centre dog seem to be waiting for that dog to go.

Finally without warning the three large dogs emerge out of the trees barking at the sheep which immediately run off in the opposite direction. The trees come to life as the startled birds take to flight along the tree line.

An older lamb is slower than the rest to respond and quickly becomes a target for one of the dogs that closes the gap quickly. The lamb runs hard for its life, but has no chance with a slow start and being in close proximity to the tree line. The dog catches it quickly by the hindquarter, dragging it down and tripping over it, rolling over and over at no time letting go of the hapless animal. The dog finally stops rolling over and savagely grabs the lamb by the neck killing it as he does so.

The second dog has already killed a young lamb and grabs an adult by the neck, dragging it down almost straight afterwards, while in the background the Alpha dog has killed one sheep and is also onto its second. The first dog that had killed the lamb earlier has successfully killed a second sheep and is chasing down a third one in the background.

In moments, one of the younger sheep is brought down at the back, its neck broken by the sharp jaws of one of the dogs. Another is brought down just ahead of that one by a dog ripping into its hind leg, dropping the hapless animal immediately.

The three dogs run rampant continuing to kill many of the sheep and badly mauling others before they finally vanish back into the tree line.

# CHAPTER THREE

The moon is low on the horizon and all is still as a six foot long dog-like animal comes out of a cave in the rocks. It stretches its long body out, yawning to reveal an unusually large bit for it's size.  It brings itself back in from its stretch and then walks off slowly, its stiff tail parallel to the ground. In the moonlight, the stripes going down its back are revealed against its grayish brown coat.

It walks off slowly sniffing its surroundings as it does. It moves past a location but comes back to it again, sniffs the ground around that spot and walks back and forwards for several seconds before it stops momentarily and then heads off in a direction, 90 degrees from where it was originally heading, following the scent of its potential prey.

The Tasmanian Tiger keeps following the trail set across the side of the rise and then finally goes down it for a time, before it stops.

There is a faint noise ahead as something moves.  Stopping, the Tasmanian Tiger sniff the air and then moves slowly forward until it gets to a covered low branch and watches as a small wallaby grazes on high grasses to it's right.  The Tasmanian Tiger moves slowly out to the right into a better position to attack the unwary wallaby.

The wallaby has limited locations with which to move towards, as there is a sharp rise behind it extending to the thick scrub to the left.

In the growing light of the early morning, the Thylacine moves closer and closer until finally it rushes its prey which pays for its slow reaction time. Its neck is snapped in one swift movement as the jaws of the Thylacine come crashing in on the neck of the wallaby.

## CHAPTER FOUR

The sun rises over a new day, peeping over the horizon as the door to the old timber cottage opens and a tall, skinny, wiry built man with grey hair steps through the door to take in the scene of a new day.  To his left the forest towers over the cottage, vanishing into the distance, while to his front stretching over to the right is semi open country with a scattering of trees and a timber shed. The sound of chooks going about their business wafts around from the left side of the cottage.

As he stands there taking in the scene, two dogs come racing over to him, jumping all around and seemingly all over him, until he tells them to sit.

The cottage door opens and a lady of similar age comes out holding two cups, steam rising out of them.  She is shorter than the man at about 5'6" to his 6'2", but also with grey hair and fair skin.

"Fine morning Mary" Jack greets his wife.

"It is a great morning Jack, here is your tea" Mary replies with as she hands him his cuppa..

"Thank you, another summer has finally gone and winter will be here fairly soon" Jack continues conversation.

As Mary speaks a short, round man can be seen coming around the corner in the distance on foot walking fast panting as if his been running.

"Been a wet autumn so far. What is Mario in a hurry about"? Mary finishes with.

Jack hands Mary his cup of tea and he steps down from the verandah and starts to walk towards the figure coming his way.

"I'll see what he wants" he tells Mary as he walks across the paddock, both his dogs following him.

Mario sees Jack coming and he starts to run, even in his exhausted state the urgency etched into his facial features. Jack sees this and indicates with his hand for Mario to slow down and walk.  Mario nods acknowledgement and starts to walk still showing urgency in his pace.

As they get to each other Mario hunches over leaning on his knees as he starts talking fast with his English laced with his thick Italian accent that is made more difficult to understand by the fact that he is struggling to draw int the breath to comfortably speak.  Finally he gets it all out.

"They have killed my sheep they have ripped my sheep apart.  Twenty gone, dead" he tells Jack.

"Who have, the Tigers"? Jack adds.

"Has too be"? Mario tells Jack putting his hands up emphasizing the point.

"When"? Jack queries.

"Last night, I just found them now.  Tigers!  I am going out there shortly to shoot them that's what I am going to do"! Mario threatens.

Jack puts his hands up to calm Mario down.

"Mario, been hunting the bastards all my life you leave that up to me.  I will get rid of this vermin, you mark my words" he tells Mario.

"Mario nods his head in thanks.

"Thank you  Jack, you a good neighbor".

"As are you Mario, come on I will give you a hand to clean up the mess they made, then I will go out looking for the Tigers" Jack tells Mario walking towards his property with him turning as he walks to wave to Mary who waves back.

Jack walks through the front door of the cottage covered in blood, Mary who is at the table darning socks looks up in surprise.

"What have you been doing"? Mary asks.

"Tigers got Mario's sheep and I helped him to dispose of them.  Sorry Mary I've got to go out and get that thing and shoot it before we all lose any more animals" Jack tells Mary apologetically.

Jack takes his shirt off as he speaks to reveal a long healed scar on his shoulder, Mary getting up to meet him and take his shirt.

"Jack, you've got to do what you've got to do. I have managed in the past and I will manage again" Mary adds in a matter of fact manner.

# CHAPTER FIVE

Andrew sits on a train as it travels through the Tasmanian wilderness, staring out of the window and occasionally smiling at the old lady opposite him who smiles back in between doing her embroidery. The two are the only two in the cabin. Finally the old lady speaks to Andrew.

"So what are you doing out here from England, just got here have you"? the old lady asks.

"Yes, I arrived yesterday morning. I am out here to obtain a Tasmanian Tiger for the London Zoo and to learn more about their environment" Andrew tells the old lady.

"You are lucky you did not leave it a few more years. Nearly all gone they are" she adds in a defeatist manner.

"I hear they are now rare and hard to come by. Protected by law now. Hopefully that will make a difference" Andrew adds.

"There are a lot of stubborn old men running farms out here. I am afraid it will not" she tells Andrew.

"You seem to know a bit about them, how is that"? Andrew asks.

"My uncle used to have one as a pet back in the 90's in his old age for a while. Docile animal, fairly skittish. It's the times I guess" she finishes with.

Andrew leans forward a bit.

"Long shot. I know but is he still alive"?

"Dear, I am his age  when he had the Tassie Tiger, no been gone a long time now, that's life I guess" she adds sentimentally.

She suddenly puts her hand out.

"Most rude of me, I am Ethel and you are"? she offers.

Andrew leans forward and shakes hands with her.

"Oh sorry most rude of me, I am Andrew. Nice to met you Ethel". Andrew adds before he leans back.

"We are almost there Andrew, pulling in to the station yard now" she tells him.

The brakes of the train screech almost on cue.

"Finally, its been a while getting here you know" he tells her as he stands up.

"Want you luggage down"? he then asks.

"Oh thank you very much" she thanks him.

Andrew gets her two bags down and one case before he gets his own down and then he sits down to see the sign say New Norfolk on the name board.

Andrew looks out of the window of the train anxiously as the train pulls up at the New Norfolk railway station. The train comes to a halt and Andrew gets up.

He puts his hand out to Ethel.

"Nice to speak to you Ethel, may see you again one day" Andrew offers as the trains guard turns up at the cabin door.

"Yes and you too Andrew, good luck with the Tiger" Ethel farewells Andrew.

Andrew picks up his pack and a bag, nod to the guard and disappears out the door immediately.

Andrew steps out on to the platform and then looks around. He sees a tall man with dark grey hair in the distance, standing on the platform searching the crowd. Andrew heads over to him and is simultaneously spotted by the other man, who also starts to walk in Andrew's direction. They both shake hands simultaneously.

"It's been awhile Andrew" the other man says.

Andrew smiles as he speaks.

"Yes Bill it has been, Palestine during the Great War. Last time I saw you was in Jerusalem at wars end. Good to see you under better circumstances".

They start to walk away from the train as they continue to talk.

"I have arranged what you need including a truck, not easy out here, but it is done. I ended up having to buy that one. All is organized, you are ready to hunt Tigers now Andrew" Bill proclaims in a cheerful manner.

" Good I do need to stretch my legs a bit now" Andrew informs Bill.

Bill laughs.

"Oh do not worry, by the time we finish you will have stretched your legs".

Bill looks up at the sky.

"Rain later I reckon, we'll see".

"Won't affect us will it"? Andrew asks Bill.

"Not today" is all Bill replies.

The two men then walk off towards a truck parked out the front of the railway station with a cage on the back of it.

# CHAPTER SIX

Jack steps down from his verandah and turns to his wife and bids her farewell.

"Not sure Mary when I will be back. Could be soon if that cloud drops a heap of rain on us".

Mary replies.

"Well be a little careful, good hunting Jack" she shouts from the verandah as Jack taps his right thigh and both dogs come straight up next to him, as the three of them head off towards the forests to the left of their home.

Jack looks up at the sky and starts muttering to himself and the dogs.

"This could be a short trip boys, don't go getting too excited. We'll see soon enough I guess".

On a rise above a track through the forest, Jack can be seen walking along an ill-defined path that favours the lower terrain. As he walks through the forest he and his two dogs are being watched by a Tasmanian Tiger. Jack and his dogs seem to be oblivious to it.

The Tasmanian Tiger turns and vanishes up the rise, away from where Jack and his two dogs are going.

Jack is stopped in the forest, boiling a billy of tea on a small fire he has made. Both his dogs are resting under a tree near him. He looks around, up in the sky and shakes his head.

"Have not seen one yet boys, only a couple of hours in though I guess. Still we should not have to go far as Mario's sheep are not far from here" Jack says to his two disinterested dogs.

Jack finally finishes his tea, flicks the remains into the forest and pours the remainder of the water on the fire, standing up as he does and then he pushes a fair amount of dirt over the fire to extinguish it before he heads off tapping his side as he does.

Jack is so used to the dogs following that he does not even check whether they are coming, he trusts that they are.

Jack walks through the forest looking for signs of Tasmanian Tigers, stopping every now and then to check out evidence on the ground to something that catches his eye. He crouches down to have a closer look and just shakes his head.

"Not a lot of luck today boys, Mario will just have to worry about his sheep a day or so longer going by what is brewing up above us"

Jack looks up as he speaks, at the dark clouds that have been building all around him through out the day.

Jack then gets up rather gingerly and starts to move on.

"Come on boys, we might as well see what we can find for another half hour or so and then call it a day. What do you reckon, good idea? I think so" Jack says to his two dogs answering for them!

Later back in the cottage Mary is cooking at the stove with the driving rain pounding on making such a racket on the roof that she barely realizes that Jack has comes through the door grumbling about the rotten luck and the rain that has ruined his hunt.

"Bloody rain soaked through and through and not a Tiger in sight. They are getting much cleverer at hiding from me, I give you the drum".

"Hello Jack, you're not going to tramp that mud and water throughout the house are you"? Mary challenges Jack.

Jack stops where he is and looks himself up and down and then over at Mary who has gone back to cooking, ignoring Jack entirely. Jack looks at the rifle he is holding and theen he looks over at the rack that it hangs on and then finally back at his clothes . He stands there looking around, lost for a few seconds before Mary smiles still not looking at him.

"Go on Jack put the rifle away and then don't tramp that mess around the house".

"Oh okay then" is the only response that Mary gets.

Jack goes and puts his rifle away as the rain gets heavier as it pounds loudly on the roof.

# CHAPTER SEVEN

Jack pulls his dray up out the front of the Trading Store marked  Rayner Trading and climbs down from the seat and starts to walk towards the front of the store when Bill shouts out from behind him to get his attention.

"Jack!

Jack walks on momentarily until Bill shouts out louder!

"Jack"!

Jack stops and turns around to see that it is Bill calling out with a younger man walking next to him.  Once Bill has Jacks attention, Bill almost runs over to him.

The only greeting from Jack is sharp tongue lashing as he snaps

"Aren't you supposed to be in the Trading Post not galivanting around the countryside no doubt gossiping like some old woman"!

Bill sarcastically replies "Yes good afternoon to you too Jack"!

Jack only grunts a reply before Bill introduces Andrew to Jack

"Jack this is Andrew, Andrew this is Jack!.

Andrew replies politely.

"Good to meet you Jack"

"Howdy", is Jacks only reply, short and curt.

"Jack we have a business deal that is right up your alley, how about coming to the pub and we'll discuss it over a beer" Bill says enthusiastically.

"I bet you have, will it take long"? Jack shoots back staring at Andrew.

"Maybe, nah it , shouldn't be too long really" Bill down plays it to Jack.

"Don't really have the time Bill" and with that he walks towards the store.

"Jack you'll need to wait for me as Andrew and I are going for a beer anyway". Bill comes back rather cheekily.

Jack looks puzzled.

"Who's manning the store"?

"Me"! Bill says with surprise.

Andrew stares at Bill, a confused look on his face.

Jack turns and walks towards the pub, mumbling a response that they just hear.

"Blackmail is unbecoming Bill, come lets go and hear this proposal before I reject it out of hand".

"You need to be open minded Jack, you'll like this one" Bill reassures Jack.

"Are you going to give me all my supplies for free from now on Bill" Jack gives as a retort, sniggering to himself as he says it.

Bill throws his arms up in the air and turns to Andrew and makes a face showing frustration.

He snaps at Jack with a cheeky tone.

"Why are you so hard to deal with Jack, snappy old bastard".

Andrew in the meantime just watches these two carry out their exchange wondering what his let himself in for as Jack replies.

I am a farmer Bill!  I cannot just ignore my Business to socialize with any errant Pom that might be wandering around the place".

Andrew glares at Jack who adds before Andrew can say anything. "Is this one of those tight arsed Poms that is going to rip me off like that mob in South Africa"?

Andrew is trying to link it all together and asks.

"South Africa"?

Bill's answer is short.

"Boer War"!

Andrew nods,

"Ahhhh"! before adding

"You'll get paid to help me find a Tasmanian Tiger for the London Zoo".

Jack stops, turns and looks at him "How much?"

Andrew responds "Enough".

Bill then cuts in "Shall we go to the pub and talk"?

Jack turns back around and walks to the pub, Andrew and Bill follow.

"We'll see"? Jack responds with skepticism thickly laid on for their benefit.

Bill, Jack and Andrew sit at a table in the corner of the bar in a local pub. Jack sits with skepticism written all over his face, waiting for one of the other two to start.

"What do you have for me"? Jack asks.

The London Zoo has charged me with finding them a Tasmanian Tiger to add to the one they already have. That is the crux of the matter and the only place to get one is here in Tasmania.

"A good Tiger is a dead one and that is that" snaps back Jack

"What, even if it is being shunted off to London never to return. What harm will that be to you Jack"?

What if you breed them and we get them back in the future"?

Bill looks at Jack with a puzzled look on his face.

"That's a stretch there Jack".

Andrew leans forward "Have you seen the London Zoo"?

Jack looks at Andrew in a non-commital manner.

Bill leans forward too, Jack responds by leaning further backwards. "It will be going to one of the most cold, miserable places god has ever made".

Andrew glares at Bill, "I would not put it quite like that".

Jack looks over at Andrew with a frown on his face "Are you kidding, I was in London during the war and saw that place. If you had of put Ned there, he would of bloody hung himself".

Jack then leans forward himself and grabs Andrew's hand and shakes it.

"Deal, if the Pommy bastard wants to put a Tiger in that godforsaken miserable place I am happy to help".

Bill sits up and smile. Good, we'll get together later and discuss when".

# CHAPTER EIGHT

Jack and Mary sit at the kitchen table opposite each other having lunch while Jack talks about the hunt for the Tasmanian Tiger.

"It should not be too hard to catch one even though they are a cunning beast.  Getting it out of the forest could be interesting with only the three of us".

Mary frowns.

"I thought it was you and the Pommy guy"?

"Bill's coming as well", Jack informs Mary.

"Good, the Pommy guy will probably walk out of the forest then?'

'Bugger shooting him they'll probably shoot me like they did to poor Breaker back in the Boer War" Jack replies as a noise can now be heard in the distance.

Both look at each other rather puzzled.

"Sounds like one of them trucks" Jack says.

Is that what it is"? Mary says  as she gets up from the table and walks to the door, Jack covering the distance fairly quickly to go out the door right behind Mary.

As they come out through the door the truck pulls up.  Andrew is driving a truck that has a tray on the back with a large metal cage on it and a couple of back packs.  Bill who sits next to Andrew smiles and waves.

Mary walks over as Jack stands back a bit, observing the truck at a distance.

Andrew climbs down from the cab as Bill vanishes out the cab on the other side.

He emerges around the truck as Jack finally comes down from the verandah and shakes hands with both men.

"You both ready for a hard slog through the forests."? Jack puts out there in a rather gruff manner.

Andrew in good humour shoots back

"We are indeed, it should be quite an adventure".

"This is not the jungles of Africa boy, and these are shy animals that we need to track down and then try to capture" Jack throws back at Andrew rather sharply.

Mary glares at Jack who sees her glaring at him and which he responds to by turning slightly away from her.

"We know what we are in for Jack" comes back Bill.

"I know you do Bill but what about the Pom with you" Jack shoots back.

"Lunch anyway" Mary pipes up with in an attempt to finish this line of conversation.

"Good idea, I am famished", Andrew proclaims while smiling, ignoring Jacks rudeness.

Seated at the kitchen table the three of them discuss the coming hunt while Mary gets Bill and Andrew some stew out of the pot that is on the stove.

Jack explains.

"The terrain is  tough with not much in the way of paths to walk through and a lot of going up and down before going up again.  We are also in their environment and they are very good at getting around.  They are not a quick animal, with a rather slow awkward walk, but are shy and will vanish at the slightest noise.  They avoid contact with man where they can.  You both need to travel light, Bill you would have already sorted that considering how many times you have travelled with me, right?"

Bill confirms this.

"Yes we are organized, with no rattles in our gear".

Andrew smiles as Jack looks at him with surprise on his face.

"We will leave at about 4 o'clock this afternoon and get ourselves an hour into the scrub, that way we are ready tomorrow morning to get on their trail" states Jack.

Both Bill and Andrew nod agreement and start eating what has been put in front of them by Mary.

# CHAPTER NINE

The three men stand out the front of Jacks cottage with their backpacks on. The dogs jump around excitedly until Jack pats his thigh and they both sit down next to him instantly. Jack then turns to his wife Mary and waves goodbye to her as she stands on the verandah watching them leave.

Andrew and Bill wave goodbye and the three of them head off to the forest on the left.

"Well let's get going and trap a Tiger to send to hell on Earth" Jack announces laughing as he says it.

"I don't know Jack we might be able to breed them and send them back in the future if your population ever becomes extinct" Andrew fires back very quickly.

Jack mumbles to himself inaudibly as Andrew winks at Bill who shakes his head in response to Andrew.

The dogs head off the moment Jack has moved ahead of them.

Mary watches them head off from the verandah before she heads back inside.

They get to the edge of the forest rather quickly and vanish into it.

"Right on the edge here aren't you Jack"? Andrew notes to the others.

"Best place to be on Earth, fought in the Boer wars and over in Gallipolli and the Western Front during the war, this is home, this is where I'll die" Jack comes back with emphatically as they continue to walk.

Later they are walking through the thick bush, Jack at the front, Bill second and Andrew to the rear. Andrew suddenly stops and puts his hands on his knees to rest his back, before he stands tall again, wipes his brow and returns to the same position, looking forward momentarily before looking down again.

Meanwhile the other two continue walking until Jack looks back to see Andrew resting where he stood. Jack looks up at the sky and then looks around the area and then drops his pack.

"This is as good a spot as any to break for the night, we'll set up camp and then rest.".

Bill nods okay and then drops his pack, stretching as it hits the ground. Andrew in the background does the same thing.

Andrew looks over at Jack, "Early start in the morning?  He asks.

"Yes, the Tigers hunt nocturnally, especially just before dawn and around dusk, so we will be active at these times as well" responds Jack.

Andrew is nodding agreement

An hour later as the day has given way to night the three of them sit eating damper and sipping a cup of tea. Jack looks over at Andrew and asks him,

"What do you know of the Tigers."?

"I know what you told us earlier, I know that they are rare now and are not seen as often as they used to be.  They seem to live solitary or in small groups, as you said they don't run well, quite ungainly actually and hunting them is now banned".

Bill sits quietly as Jack and Andrew talk.

"The scourge of the farmers they are, their demise will be a long time coming" Jack comes back with.

Andrew looks over at him.

"They are a unique animal with the look of a dog, yet the ancestry of the marsupials.  They do share similar traits with dogs.  They fulfill the same niche as the dogs do in other parts of the world".

Jack frowns as he responds "We lose a lot of sheep to them each year".

Bill finally cuts in

"Are we going to find it easy to get one or is it going to be hard"?

"It will not be easy, as I said they are shy and avoid man where possible. We need to ascertain those in the area and then move to set traps for one. You have that dart gun of yours there Andrew"? Jack proclaims with a question at the end of the comment.

Andrew responds.

"Yes I have and we can also make a trap as well, I have a set of plans and I also have what we need to make one".

Jack smiles.

"Good you are prepared, that will help".

Bill finally stretches.

"Well gentlemen it is time for a good sleep".

Jack nods agreement as Andrew sits not responding, getting a note book out and starts to write some notes.

"I'll write a few notes before going to bed".

# CHAPTER TEN

Later in the night a Thylacine is hunting, searching, stopping to sniff the air every now and then before it moves off again in a direction. It hears noise to its right and then heads that way slowly and methodically.

Cautiously it moves slowly, expecting to come up on something at any moment. It stops, sniffs the area and then goes to ground with its nose smelling for a scent. It seems to have no scent to find and then moves on carrying out the same patterns as it does so.

The camp site is quiet as the three men sleep, the dogs are sleeping either side of Jack. The dog to Jacks left suddenly puts its head up before it sits up attentively, followed by the second dog which does the same thing.

Both dogs start to move around the spot before they both start to howl.

Jack who is in his swag, sits bolt upright and responds very quickly grabbing his rifle.

"Where is it boys, where is it" Jack asks his dogs as he gets out of his swag and starts a visual inspection of the area.

Bills sits up in his swag while Andrew who has a canopy up over his, also sits up.

Andrew bleary eyed and not with it asks.

"What is going on"?

Jack is quick and sharp in a low voice that Andrew understands real quickly.

"Shut up, Tiger in the area".

Andrew is looking around from his position, while the dogs continue to howl.

The Thylacine hears the noise of the dogs howling, stops, listens momentarily and then changes direction away from the howling of the dogs. This time the Thylacine is not sniffing or searching, it is just moving out of the area as quickly as its ungainly trait allows it.

As it moves away the howling gets quieter in the distance, eventually almost blending into the background before it seems to stop altogether.

Some time later the dogs have finally stopped howling and the three men stand around in the centre of the camp looking around, both Jack and Bill still have their rifles at hand.

Andrew asks the question

"What caused that entire ruckus".

"That my friend is the calling card of a Tiger when one is around dogs are known to howl like that.  They are totally different types of animals too each other despite the visual similarities to one another.  The two do not get on" replies Jack.

Bill confirms this.

"Andrew its true, if one is around all the dogs do that".

"Amazing, how intriguing" Is Andrews only response to that as he heads back to his swag

Bill and Jack stand watching Andrew vanish without any further ado.

Jack turns to go back to his swag and the dogs have already settled down to their respective positions.  Jack smiles.

"Look they both agree with the bloody Pom, traitors, both of you".

Bill says nothing and goes back to his own swag,

Both are back to bed within moments.

It does not take long for all to be quiet again, only the normal noises of the night can now be heard, the crickets now have their forest back and the chorus starts again.

## CHAPTER ELEVEN

It is early morning, the sun is not yet up, but the morning has lightened and the three men are moving through the forest with the dogs getting ahead of Jack as they sniff the ground out ahead of them.

Jack looks back to see that Bill and Andrew are right behind him, but neither are as sure footed as he is, Andrew in particular is tripping over things rather clumsily.

"A heard of elephants would be quieter traipsing through here than you two ballerina's" Jack says rather sharply.

Bill looks up and trips over instantly just to prove the point.

Jack turns and keeps walking as Andrew helps Bill up.

"Point taken" mutters Jack to himself.

"You alright there Bill"? asks Andrew with concern in his voice.

Bill stands up rather gingerly and looks forward to the vanishing Jack.

"Yes I am fine, thanks for the hand there Jack" he changes tone as he thanks Jack rather sarcastically.

Jack acknowledges with a wave of a hand and keeps walking.

Andrew's eyes follow Jack around the corner, "Cantankerous old bastard isn't he"?

"Jack will never change" Bill comes back with as he heads off rather gingerly.

The sun is now filtering through the forest canopy, the dogs are now well ahead of Jack on the trail of something up ahead.

"Jack pats his thigh firmly, one of the dogs further behind the other stops and looks back. Jack pats his thigh again and whistles for it to come back to him. The other dog that was further ahead seems not to hear Jack and keeps going.

Once the dog reaches Jack he rewards it with something out of his pocket and then start to move quicker through the undergrowth of the forest.

"Good boy, good boy"!

The dog stays with Jack maintaining its station to Jacks right.

Andrew watches Jack's urgency and then asks Bill

"What is the urgency here Bill, if the dog catches up with the Tasmanian Tiger want it just keep it pinned down for us"?

Bill shakes his head no.

"If that is a full grown Tiger out there Jacks dog could be killed before we get to it, Jacks lost quite a few dogs over the years to the Tigers" Bill tells Andrew.

I thought they would be a good match for the Thylacine's"? Andrew comes back with as Bill picks up the pace a little.

"No they are not, not one on one anyway" replies Bill.

Ahead, Jack can now be heard calling out to his dog.

Is the dog partially deaf"? queries Andrew.

"Yes it is" but a favourite of Jacks too, had it for quite some time now.

They move through the bush in the direction Jack has vanished in.

A single shot rings out in the air startling Andrew.

"Jack is trying to get the dogs attention with a shot, is all you are hearing I suspect" Bill reassures Andrew.

"Or they have caught up with the Tiger"?

"No he will be trying to get the dogs attention" Bill comes back with.

Andrew and Bill finally catch up with Jack as he is releasing the second dog.

"Go boy, go, go find him" Jack shouts out as the dog vanishes through the bush.

"Didn't come back"? asks Andrew.

"No bloody thing, nearly deaf as a post, come lets follow them" is Jacks reply as the three of them head off at pace.

The Tasmanian Tiger hears the noise coming through the bush, turning it braces itself.

As it stands waiting, the first dog comes around the corner of a huge tree and is confronted by the Tasmanian Tiger waiting for it.

It is over quickly as the Tasmanian Tiger stands braced, rocking from side to side.  The dog rushes into the Tasmanian Tiger.  As it launches itself at the Tasmanian Tiger, the Tiger swings out and comes down over the dog taking the top of its skull clean off.

There is one high yelp from the stricken dog.

The dog is dead before it hits the ground.

The Tasmanian Tiger heads off through the bush, vanishing quickly as it melts into its surroundings.

Jack can hear a dog barking ahead of him, he breaks into a run nearly knocking himself out on a low hung branch as he ducks to avoid it.

He finally drops his pack and is gone running as fast as he can, coming around a corner he sees one of his dogs laying still on the ground, a pool of blood around its head region.  The other dog sits near it quietly.

Jack halts and stares at his dog shaking his head.

"No! No not another one" is all he says as he moves in next to his dog and collapses onto the ground.

He looks the dog over thoroughly as Andrew and Bill come around the large tree and stop in their tracks, Andrew holding onto Jacks pack.  He puts it down.

"Is there anything" he stops as he speaks when he sees the massive head injury that the dog has.

Jack looks up at Andrew and then back at his dog as Bill comes up next to Jack and crouches down.

Andrew can you get the billy going while we attend to Jacks dog" Bill asks Andrew.

Andrew nods a yes and then takes his pack over next to Jacks and heads into the bushes.

# CHAPTER TWELVE

Bill and Jack stand over the fresh grave where Jacks dog is now buried.

Jack does not say a thing as he strokes his other dog on the head.

Bill looks over to Jack before he leaves Jack alone.

"Sorry mate" is his parting comment.

Jack nods a thanks and stands with his remaining dog next to him.

"Its been a long day dog and a hard one, lets see if we can get some shut eye. We got a Tiger to kill tomorrow"!

At that he turns around not waiting for Bill and commences to walk back to camp. Bill follow him with his eyes while realizing tonight's campfire may not be great one and tomorrow definitely will not be. After a short contemplation he too turns around and heads off towards the camp area.

The next morning Andrew is leans over and checks the billy which is hanging form a tripod over the fire as Bill arrives at the camp fire.

Without looking up from the billy Andrew greets Bill!

"Morning Bill, billy's nearly done"!

Bill nods agreement

Morning Andrew, sleep well"?

Andrew stands up taking in the still dark morning sky bristling with stars with a cold breeze blowing in from the south. As Bill is assessing the day to come Andrew makes an observation out of the blue.

"Pretty attached to his dogs isn't he'? Andrew says to Bill as he gets next to him.

"He works with them daily and relies on them, he gets attached" replies Bill.

Andrew turns his attention back to the fire getting the billy off the flame and coals going over to the three tin mugs to his left on a log. Then he pours the tea.

"Cup of tea is ready" he calls out.

Jack finally gets out of his swag and comes over and joins them, taking a cup from Andrew when Andrew offers him one and sits down saying nothing.

Jack sits not saying a thing, only poking the fire with a stick as Bill is looking up to the sky.

Bill looks over at Jack and realizes that Jack is still upset over yesterdays events, still dwelling on it, simmering inside so he decides to leave him alone and turns his attention back to the sky!

After some observation of the sky he tries to use the coming day to break the ice and get them refocused on their task at hand!

"We should avoid the rain by the looks of it" Bill proclaims.

"That would be good, be nice to avoid it all together if you ask me" Andrew responds with.

Bill stares at him.

"You're English and you want to avoid rain, that's like a Melbournian telling someone he's never seen rain before. You will get soaked at least once over the next few days, probably more actually" Bill comes back with.

"Melbournian"? asks Andrew.

Before Bill can respond Jack cuts in.

"I am going to kill that vermin, the deal is off. You can either join me or bugger off, either suits me"!

Andrew and Bill look at him with stunned looks on their faces.

"Jack you have a deal here, you don't just break a deal like that" Bill shoots back quickly and firmly.

"I just have" Jack snaps back.

"Are you for real"? Andrew adds.

Jack looks up before standing and picking up the billy and pouring the remainder of the water onto the fire.

Andrew gets splashed by the water and stands up sharply.

"You have to follow through with this bargain Jack" Andrew reiterates to Jack.

"Why"? is the response as Jack gets up and walks over to his backpack and puts it on.

"It is what you agreed to" Bill adds.

Jack has his backpack on and goes to pick up his rifle as Bill comes over and cuts in front of him.

Jacks dog starts to growl at Bill.

Bill looks down at it and points.

"If that thing goes for me you will loose another dog very quickly" shoots Bill back at Jack who very quickly pats his thigh and the dog come over and sits down.

Andrew has his pack on and hands Bill his.

Thanks" replies Bill.

Andrew cuts in again.

"Look Jack, we are both very sorry for the loss of your dog, but I want this animal and what does it really matter to you if it is shot or whether I take it back to that godforsaken dungeon back in London".

"Jack looks him in the eyes.

"It matters, it matters, I want it dead.

"No this is a knee jerk reaction Jack, I know how you think, known you for a while now.  I have never seen you break a deal, this cannot be the first. You were only saying yourself the other day that these animals will be gone in twenty to thirty years, Andrew may not get another shot at this" Bill cuts in with toning down the emphasis in his voice as he speaks.

Andrew looks at Bill and then at Jack.

"Jack I need this to go ahead.  While I do not want to look for another guide I will and I will get what I want.  I don't care whether I pay you or another, now are we getting on our way"

Jack shifts his feet slightly looking down then over to his dog before he pushes past them both mumbling to himself.

"Come on you Pommy bastard and Pommy lover lets get going".

Andrew looks up at the sky and mouths "Thank you lord" before he starts walking behind Jack.

Bill smiles and follows up the rear.

## CHAPTER THIRTEEN

It is now late in the day and not a word is being spoken as the three men and one dog quietly walk through the forest, the dog walking along ahead of Jack searching for a scent. As they get to a creek crossing their path, the rushing of the water and the sounds of the birds the only sounds that can be heard.

Jack indicates to Bill and Andrew to prop where they are and wait with hand signals.  Then he pats his thigh and the dog comes over to him and walks next to him as Jack walks up the creek line without going in the water for some distance, vanishing briefly before he comes back down the creek line again and past their position.

Jack ignores both of them as he continues to look for signs of the Tasmanian Tiger.

Jack vanishes again in the distance.

Bill and Andrew wait with only the noises of the creek and the forest around them.

Bill whispers.

"Apparently during the Boer War, Jack and his brother Ted were pretty good scouts catching a few of the Boer out with their skill.  Jack is probably the best bushman in this part of the country, just a little bit eccentric every now and then.  He also has more bias opinions than any other person I know".

"I met a lot of Australians in Palestine, all were hard nosed and damn good bushmen generally" Andrew adds.

Suddenly in the distance there is a sharp whistle that is repeated twice, both Bill and Andrew get up and come as quick as they can with the backpack on their backs.

As they get close, Jack indicates for them not to go across his front but to come in behind him.

They look where he is pointing.

There are long paw prints in the ground that look dog like.

Jack looks up smiling.

"That my friend is the tracks of a Tiger heading up that way", triumph in his voice.

Andrew crouches down and checks out the prints that are in the mud.

"So that is definitely a Thylacine"? asks Andrew.

"It is indeed" Jack states with Bill nodding agreement behind him.

"How do you tell" asks Andrew.

"Similar to a dogs paw print but the rear foot print is generally longer than a dogs and the print pattern left are slightly different. The front foot print has two pad prints and the the toe print is wider than a dogs with a wider forward spread too. After a time you do get used to picking them out. It becomes second nature." Jack explains.

Andrew listens intently to Jacks explanation and realizes that Jack is quite an expert on the Thylacine, someone he can learn a fair bit from if he gets the chance.

"Thanks Jack, you know them well don't you"?

Jack nods a yes as he relies

"I have been tracking and hunting them for a long time".

Andrew stays crouched looking at the prints studying pulling out a note book and drawing the prints in silence as moves up next to Bill joining him in studying what they can see of the sky amid the thick forests only discernable because of the creek.

They both study the sky and the long shadows of the trees on the creek, Bill looking over at Jack who is studying the direction that the Tasmanian Tiger went in.

Bill breaks the silence as Andrew continues to sketch the foot prints.

"Camp here for the night"?

Jack nods yes.

"Not a bad spot, might even be able to use this as our base. We will set up over there" he tells his two companions.

Andrew is looking around the area and does not seem to be listening to the other two until Bills taps him on the shoulder.

"Andrew we will camp here for the night".

Andrew looks up.

"Oh thanks Bill" he comes back with and then gets up and follows Bill over to where they are going to camp.

# CHAPTER FOURTEEN

That night the three are around the camp fire with Jacks last dog laying next to Jack sleeping.

Jack finally looks up at Andrew who is writing in a notebook by the camp fire.

"You up to building that cage trap tomorrow while I scout the area"? Jack asks Andrew.

"Yes I have what I need to build it.  I will take all day though I suspect". Andrew replies with.

Bill who is listening adds.

"I will give you a hand tomorrow Andrew".

"Thanks" Andrew acknowledges Bills offer.

"Jack you going to find a location for this trap"? asks Bill.

Jack nods a yes as he replies.

"I will  prepare the materials and we will assemble it at the location, otherwise it will be awkward to get to location".

Andrew smiles and replies "Will do".

The conversation dies again there as Andrew goes back to his notebook, Jack  stands up and pours himself another tea while Bill starts poking the fire.

Andrew suddenly looks up at Bill.

"Who are Melbournians"?

Bill smiles.

"Our brethren who live in Melbourne Victoria or as we used to call them Mexicans"!

Andrew nods an acknowledgement before a puzzled look washes over his face.

"Mexicans"? he queries.

"I am from Wilcannia in New South Wales, Victoria is south of the border, that makes them Mexicans.

"Ah" is Andrews reply.

"Jack who has sat down again comes back with.

The rivalry on the northern island of Tasmania is unnecessarily fierce, rather childish if you ask me.

Andrew who is now looking down at Jack's dog asks Jack.

"How long to train a dog to do what you want them to do"?

"A few years, I get them as pups, these two I got through Mario and a few others in the past.  It takes a lot of time and they don't come with me on hunts for awhile, sure way to get them killed" Jack replies as he pats his dogs head.

"You lost many over the years" Andrew continues.

"A lot one way or the other.  Not as many now and this is the smallest number I have had. Normally I have four to six, but with the Tiger bounties gone now I am not out here as much as I used to be". Jack seems to be dropping into deep thought as they speak.

"The Tasmanian Tigers were prolific in the past"? Andrew asks again.

"Yes cleared out of some areas pretty quick, but here and in some of the other remote areas where there are few people, who knows how many survived.  Old Ethel in town her uncle used to keep one as a pet, he used to have a soft spot for them.  He used to reckon we were all paranoid.  He used to claim it was mainly stray dogs that took our sheep, silly old coot.  What would he know'? Jack finishes with.

"Met Ethel on the train, she told me her uncle used to keep one as a pet, do you remember it or did you see him with it"? Andrew continues to question Jack.

"I was young back then it would hide when you came around but if you went past his place you could see it sitting at his feet like a silly bloody dog in the afternoons.  Made for each other they seemed to be". Jack responds.

Bill suddenly asks a question.

"What happened to it"?

"I reckon the Tiger died one night and the silly old bugger went a few weeks later.  Could be wrong, good story anyway"? Jack adds.

Jack stands up.

"Well, see you tomorrow, bed for an old fellow like me" and he is gone.

"Catch you tomorrow Jack, Bill farewells Jack for the night.

"See you Jack Andrew says goodnight to Jack and drifts back to his notebook while Bill goes back to poking the fire with a stick.

# CHAPTER FIFTEEN

Deeper in the forest, a Tasmanian Tiger is moving very slowly and is totally focused on the scrub just in front of it.

Slowly, one foot after another it moves quietly, stopping if it makes the slightest noise.

Ahead the wallaby is eating grasses under a tree, moving slowly as it does with no pattern to its wanderings following its whims eating the grasses not showing the alertness it should to stay alive.

It suddenly moves a few hops back towards the Tasmanian Tiger which stops momentarily.

The wallaby seems to be oblivious to its plight and the pending attack by the Tasmanian Tiger.

The wallaby moves again slightly to its left, leaving a clear path between it and the Tasmanian Tiger.  The Tasmanian Tiger launches itself at the wallaby rushing it in its awkward way.

The wallaby attempts to get away swinging out to its right but it is too slow and the Tasmanian Tiger is all over it, its large wide open jaws coming down over the top of the wallabies neck snapping it in an instant.

Without wasting time it starts to eat its meal nervously, looking around constantly as it does.

#

In the pre-dawn light the Tasmanian Tiger comes down cautiously out of the forest onto the creek line, moving slowly, stopping to check its surroundings before moving up to the

edge of the creek.

It checks the surroundings closely sniffing the air, checking the scent on the ground and looking closely up and down the creek before it goes to the creeks edge and then just as cautiously it crosses the river.

In the distance in the pre dawn light, the glow of the camp fire of the three hunters can be made out, but with the wind directions right, the Tasmanian Tiger crosses safely.  On crossing to the other side, it moves into the forest, quickly vanishing without being seen from across the river.

Once in the bush the Tasmanian Tiger stops and watches the scene across the river of the three hunters sitting around the fire and the dog resting near one of the hunters.  It loses interest in the scene and melts into its surroundings, heading back up the rise of the thickly wooded hill.

# CHAPTER SIXTEEN

Andrew, Bill and Jack sit around the fire in the morning, quietly eating damper and having a cup of tea.

"While I am out today I will do some hunting to supplement our food supply" states Jack.

Andrew surveys the area around their camp site.

"We should not have too many difficulties finding the right timbers here to make our trap." Andrew tells the others.

Jack gets up, throws the remains of his cup of tea into the bush and picks up his rifle.

"Well I will be off then and get this day started.  I am looking for evidence of the Tigers in the area and the best location for us to set up the traps" Jack explains to Bill and Andrew.

"We'll be around here all day I suspect getting ourselves organized" Bills tells Jack.

Jack and his dog head off towards the tracks that they found the evening before and then once the dog has the trail they vanish into the bushland that rises above them.

Bill looks over towards the forest.

"I will target the large frame pieces with my axe".

"I will obtain the remainder of what we need then" responds Andrew.

Bill then gets up as Andrew goes through his backpack and pulls out a set of folded sheet of paper.

"Should we get started then"? asks Andrew.

"We should indeed. We'll take a fair amount of the day to prepare this trap.  Let's hope we have it set up tonight". Bill comes back with.

Andrew heads over to his backpack and sifts through it, getting out a small saw while Bill gets an axe from his backpack and heads off into the forest around the camp.

"Be seeing you Andrew" Bill proclaims as he vanishes into the forest.

Andrew looks up before responding.

"Okay Bill, catch you later".

#

Andrew and Bill are assembling the timber of their trap into order in preparation for putting the parts together.

Andrew asks Bill.

"So Bill you were telling me a little about Jack, not the talkative type is he"?

"Not at all.  Grew up in these parts as he said and as I told you he went off to fight in South Africa during the Boer War as did one of his brothers. I believe his brother was killed out there."

"Older than Jack or younger"? Andrew asks.

Bill responds "older"

Andrew asks "Does he have any children?

"Two boys and a girl.  The girl lives in New Norfolk with another of Jack's brothers and goes to school there, while one son is in the navy and the other has joined the police force. He is stationed in the north of the state I think" Bill finishes outlining Jacks life and Andrew does not ask any more questions.

#

That evening Jack, Andrew and Bill stand back from the box style trap that Andrew and Bill have built.

Jack climbs into the trap, lays the bait and ensures that it cannot be removed by tying it into place at the rear of the trap.

"There, you are ready to go"! Jack declares as they admire their handy work.

"We may take a little time to get one but they are definitely out there somewhere" Jack adds.

"Come on we had better get back to camp and leave the area before we scare any potential prey off with our continued presence" Jack tells Andrew and Bill heading off as he talks.

They both follow him away from the trap.

## CHAPTER SEVENTEEN

By the morning Jack, Andrew and Bill are walking back to the trap in the pre-dawn low light.

Getting closer they can hear the sounds of an animal in the trap, Andrew who has overtaken Jack to take the lead looks back excited.

"I think we might have one"! exclaims Andrew.

"The impatience of it, I think it might be a Devil myself" Jack adds.

You mean a Tasmanian Devil"?

"Yes" Jack gives back as an answer.

"Bad tempered black little animals in nature and color" Bill declares.

As they come into view of the trap, Jack clarifies.

'They eat anything and everything, fur, bones and flesh, struth the little bastards would eat your boots and stinky socks too I am sure".

The Devil is pacing up and down and stops to growl and snarl at the three men as it sees them.

"Not very happy is it"? Andrew adds sarcastically.

They stop at the cage and Jack lifts his gun up and aims at the animal, when Andrew looks over.

He immediately grabs the barrel of the rifle and pushes it down.

"No, let it be Jack" Andrew says with urgency in his voice.

Jack drops the rifle, looks over at him and turns to walk back to camp.

"Where are you going"?  Andrew queries.

By now Bill has started to follow him.

"Bill"? Andrew adds as he notices him also leaving.

"I can get it out of there easy using the .303 method or you can stick you hand in there and get him out." Jack adds dryly as he vanishes around the corner.

Andrew puts his hands on his hips and stares at the snarling, grumpy little animal.

"Well let's get this over with Jack hey. Jack, yes great name for you old boy, damn apt too" Andrew proclaims rather buoyantly.

#

Jack and Bill are sitting around the fire as the sky is getting darker and dimmer as the clouds roll in.

Jacks dog is nowhere to be seen.

Jack is looking up at the sky.

"Rain I suspect by midday.  Not doing a lot of searching today I give you the drum".  Jack tells Bill.

Bill looks up and around in response.

"Just put some canvas cover up and watch the day go by I would guess". Bill says in a rather matter of fact manner.

As they discuss the plans, Andrew comes around the corner with something wrapped around his arm.

Damn that bloody thing; are all Jacks as grumpy and cantankerous as the two I have met here"? Andrew grumbles as he gets to them.

Bill and Jack look up at him with confusion on their faces and then they look at each other before Jack looks back up to him.

"What do you mean by that"?

Andrew gets himself a cup of tea and sits down as he speaks.

"Oh well it was grumbling so much and being all snarly and just damn unfriendly that the only name that suited it was Jack.  So I named it Jack and it had a red hot go when I got it out of the trap too" Andrew tells them both.

Bill takes a sip of his tea smiling to himself and Jack turns back to the fire, notices Bills reaction and responds.

"Bloody Poms, presumptuous bastards and what are you giggling about like a little girl"? Jack snaps at them both.

Andrew is busy tending his arm ignoring Jack.

Andrew then looks up and around.

"Jack where is your dog"? Andrew queries."

"Wandering around somewhere in the area I suspect" Jack replies rather casually.

"As dusk comes around we will need to see if we can snare ourselves a small marsupial to act as bait for a Tiger.  Did not think a dead animal, or a portion there of would work". Jack tells his two companions.

"Do they only eat fresh meat'? Andrew asks rather surprised.

Jack nods as he answers.

"Yes seem too, otherwise they would be easier to get and we would have them gone by this".

They sit in silence momentarily before Bill gets up.

"I will get the canvas to put up".

# CHAPTER EIGHTEEN

That evening in constant drizzle the trap is set again with a small wallaby secured in the trap.

Jack, who is in the trap pats the wallaby on the head and apologizes.

"Sorry mate, they are fussy buggers and don't like their meat already dead, so it has to be the likes of you.

Jack then backs out of the trap, moves over and stands back with Bill and Andrew.

"Well let's hope this nets us a Tiger without any more kafuffle". Bill tells Andrew and Jack.

Andrew turns and walks away.

"Hope we have more luck tonight then".

Jack and Bill turn and follow him down as the rain increases.

#

Walking around the rough path that has now been created by their many trips back and forth to the trap, Jack catches a shape in the distance next to his swag under the canvas that has been erected.

Jack stops momentarily and then breaks into a run just as Bill and Andrew notice the same thing.

"No, not another one"! Jack mumbles to himself.

Bill and Andrew run over to the covering as well.

On the ground, Jack has knelt down next to his stricken dog and is stroking it's head as he checks over its wounds.

It has a blood stain high near its neck and blood on the ground around this area and a severe wound to its hindquarter as well, which is also bleeding.

The dog's breathing is heavy and labored.

"Is he going to be alright"? Bill asks Jack as he kneels down next to the stricken dog.

"Poor bastard is done for I think, the next couple of hours will tell"? Jack states.

Andrew goes over to his pack and takes out a bag and starts to sift through it, taking out some bandaging and then gets his tin plate and goes over to Jack.

"I will get hot water and we'll see what we can do for it, can't promise anything". Andrew states as he starts to look over the animal.

Jacks looks at him.

"What do you know about looking after animals"?

Since the end of the war it is what I have been doing or assisting with since getting a position at the London Zoo" Andrew tells Jack who does not respond and just turns his attention back to his dog.

Andrew looks over the wounds closely.

"Hell, he has taken a hiding from something"? Mumbles Andrew as he continues to work on the dog.

Without looking up Jack keeps talking, challenging Andrew.

"You know a dog of this size will only have this sort of injuries from one type of animal don't you"?

"Or another dog"? adds Andrew staring Jack in the eyes.

"No, Jack is probably right out here Andrew, it will be a Tasmanian Tiger, probably a big male" Bill comes back in support of Jack.

Later during the night Jack has moved his dog nearer the fire and is sitting with it as Andrew is pouring a tea, which once he has finished doing, he brings to Jack and hands to him.

"How is he going Jack"? Andrew asks.

Jack shakes his head as he takes the cup of tea.

"Thanks, no good, he is as good as gone I would say".

"Lets hope your wrong Jack" Andrew adds as he stands there momentarily waiting for some form of response from Jack.

Jack is totally focused on his dog and does not look up or acknowledge Andrew again.

Andrew goes back to the fire and joins Bill who shakes his head.

## CHAPTER NINETEEN

The Tasmanian Tiger leaves its den and weaves through the thick forest undergrowth until it reaches the creek.

It cautiously goes to the edge of the creek and takes a drink before it carefully crosses the creek and moves up through the forest on the other side.

The eerie sounds of two Tasmanian Devils fighting nearby stops the Tasmanian Tiger in its tracks, it stops listens and then moves off again deeper into the forest.

The Tasmanian Tiger turns for that direction tracking cautiously, sniffing the air before it turns and changes directions walking at a forty five degree angle away from the fighting Devils for a little while before he turns back in for the noise. As the Tasmanian Tiger nears the spot, it slows down, cautiously moving forward.

Ahead the noise of the two Devils fighting stops, the Tasmanian Tiger still moving cautiously until it peers through the bush. There is now nothing there!

The Tasmanian Tiger steps out into the area where the fighting took place and starts sniffing around, eventually finding a wet red patch on the grass.

It follows the scent for awhile until the rain starts coming down again and it seems to lose the scent.

The Tasmanian Tiger stops, turns and changes direction, stopping moments later to sniff around. He smells the air and then changes direction, going up a rise and then turning to its left, going across the rise until it then turns and goes back down the rise at a 45 degree angle.

The Tasmanian Tiger moves down the rise again until the land flattens out and it moves back to the creek and to the edge of the water where it seems to lose the scent and then it goes up and down the creek searching the embankment.

The Tasmanian Tiger hears some noise nearby and investigates the sound, finding a possum scratching around on the ground it moves around to a slightly better position and then launches itself at it. The possum is too quick for the Tasmanian Tiger and scurries up a tree before it can be grabbed and turned into a meal.

On failing to get the possum, it turns around and heads back down to the tree line and then it props and watches the creek line.

With no noise, it cautiously moves out again from the bushes and back to searching for the scent of what it was following.

The splashes created by a lone Platypus makes the Tasmanian Tiger freeze and then move towards the bush again, but with no follow up sounds it goes back to what it was doing and goes back to its search for its prey.

# CHAPTER TWENTY

It is early morning with the first hints of a new day, in the sky that barely breaks through the thick Tasmanian forest. Andrew can be made out stirring up the fire again while behind him in the bushes a dark shape can be made out watching him.

Jack rolls over in his swag and sees the shape with the growing realization, surprise washes over his face as he recognizes a Tasmanian Tiger watching the camp. He slowly reaches for his gun with slow movements.

Andrew in the background is oblivious to this and continues to work around the fire making damper.

Andrew makes a sudden movement to his left that startles the Tasmanian Tiger and it disappears into the bush.

Jack gets up quickly, surprising Andrew as he flies off after the Tasmanian Tiger, rifle in hand.

Andrew watches him fly towards the bush and stop at the edge.

Bill sits up and looks around, Andrew is standing by the fire looking confused and Jack is standing at the edge of the scrub, rifle in hand straining to see into the darkness.

"What is going on"? Bill asks.

Andrew is first to reply.

"I am not sure, Jack just flew off to the edge of the forest and then stopped and has been breaking his neck to see deeper into the forest".

Jack spins around.

"I saw it! I saw it, a Tiger watching us through the bush"?

Jack walks back towards the fire, but stops when he see's his dog breathing heavily near his swag.

Bill looks at the dog and sees it is still breathing.

"Still alive"! Bill comments.

"Yes, but for how long"? Jack adds as he puts his rifle down and checks his dog over.

Behind him, Bill gets out of his swag and goes over to the fire, grabbing his shoes as he does.

"I am going to shoot that Tiger and get rid of it and we'll find you another". Jack tells Andrew.

Andrew looks over at him startled.

"What, we have one in the area that we will get with patience, instead you want to drag this out just to satisfy some vague sense of revenge." Shoots back Andrew angrily.

Jack stands up moving closer to Andrew.

"Vague sense of vengeance, look at the condition of my dog. Does that look vague?  Does it"?  Jack says angrily.

Bill runs his hands through his hair and mumbles to himself.

"This is going to be a long day"

He paces up and down as Andrew and Jack continue on at each other.

"What does it matter to you if that animal goes to London or another that may be a week or two away.  I am not guaranteed of even finding another one and you know that" Andrew shouts back raising his voice.

"That animal dies, do you hear that,"! Jack shouts back just as loud.

Bill finally waves his hands in the air and snaps at them both.

"I am going to check the trap and let you two fucking idiots kill each other here without any witnesses or I may just shoot both of you, grow up"! He is then gone storming off into the bush with no shoes on.

He comes back leaving them standing there watching him as he grabs his boots and storms off.

He swings back around.

"And don't spoil the tea with your blood when you kill each other, or my swag" and he is gone.

They both turn their attention to each other glaringly again at each other as a momentary standoff takes place before Jack storms off after Bill.

Andrew shakes his head and paces up and down mumbling to himself.

"Annoying old bastard.  I should shoot you myself".

He then finally heads off himself for the trap.

# CHAPTER TWENTY ONE

Andrew comes around the corner and sees another devil in the trap and nothing left of the wallaby except a few bits and pieces.

Bill and Jack look around at Andrew as he turns up showing his annoyance at another Devil in the trap.

"Can't you guys vanish for one day and leave the fucking trap alone". Andrew mutters to himself in frustration.

Jack says.

".303 method or yours"?

"Andrew snaps back.

"Mine".

Bill turns and walks off.

"Jacks method is a lot easier, I'd recommend it".

Jack stands and waits momentarily.

Andrew looks at the snarling black ball and indicates for Jack to join Bill.

Once Jack and Bill are out of the way he goes up to the trap.

"Is that you Jack?  as he looks the animal over.

"You know I reckon it might be, same or similar markings!  Ahhhhh you idiot!  It is isn't it.  Next time he can use the .303 method got it"!

Andrew then takes off his jacket and goes to the front of the cage.

\#

When Andrew finally gets back to the camp he notices that Jack is gone and then he looks down at the spot where the dog was laying.

He looks up at Bill who shakes his head and then turns back to pulling Andrew's damper out of the fire.

Andrew comes up next to him.

"Dead"? is all he asks.

Bill nods agreement and Andrew nods.

\#

Jack comes back through the forest and takes a seat next to the fire without offering a word to the other two.

Bill looks over at him but fails to get eye contact while Andrew ignores him altogether.

"Another wet day by the looks"? Bill offers.

The response is nothing initially.

"Going to sit here all day and sulk, both of you"? Bill tries a new tact.

Andrew looks up finally and responds.

"I would not mind going out and seeing if we can find evidence of the Tiger for scientific purposes"

Bill nods agreement and Jack finally speaks up

"I would like to find the others for future reference and once you are gone I will come back and finish a few others off.

Andrew looks over at Jack.

"Their numbers have been dropping rapidly over the last few decades. They will be gone without your help now probably, not enough left I would imagine to maintain the species. Once a species gets too scattered and not enough left their numbers seem to drop off quickly after a certain point. That's one line of thinking anyway. The Tasmanian Tiger seems to bare that one out. Why not let the rest live their days out or give them a chance to survive"?

"You should only ever kill for two reasons, one for food and two to get rid of vermin. They are the latter and therefore they need to go. Is it fair, probably not, but that is what I do, I hunt and even if they are on the edge, I do intend on pushing them over. I will not regret getting rid of them" Jack explains.

"Your choice I guess" Andrew adds as he gets up to walk away.

Jack stands up.

"But in the in the meantime I will help you find them for whatever study you want. Coming Bill"?

Bill stands up.

"Beats watching you two kill each other."

Bill puts the fire out as the other two grab a few items and then wait.

The three vanish into the bush in single file behind Jack.

Bill thinking to himself as he follows up behind them that Jack is far more subdued this time around.  Depressed he guesses?

"Poor bastard" he mutters to himself as he continues to traipse along behind them.

# CHAPTER TWENTY TWO

Jack stops as he sees a low branch, studies it and beckons Andrew to come over and he points at the branch.

"Tiger fur caught in that broken edge".

Andrew comes forward and studies it before he takes it out and takes a small paper bag out of a pack he is carrying and puts it in.

"Thanks, I will study that later".

He then looks at Jack.

"Are we following one"?

Jack nods yes.

"As we have discussed numbers are noticeably dropping now, once they were every where, not now".

Bill adds.

"You can still find one here and there or in places like this, but it is rare now".

They now get up and Jack indicates a direction and then he heads off up a rise and then parallel with the rise.

Later the three are seated leaning against a tree each taking a break as the sun breaks through the gloom of the cloud cover.

Jack looks at Andrew.

"So you have studied them, yes"?

Andrew nods yes as he swallows and then speaks.

"Yes I have, this trip is part of that study I guess".

"What can you tell us"? Jack asks.

"The stuff you already know that they are nocturnal, shy animals with a restricted gait. They generally prefer their meat fresh and to make their own kills. They can bear up to four joeys and seem to live for only about 10 years or less. They also live in pairs or singularly and appear to be much maligned by the settlers in the outer districts of Tasmania". Andrew tells them.

Jack responds quickly.

"I have lived all my life in this region except for my periods of military service in the Boer war and after in the Great War and I can tell you these animals have been taking a large number of sheep for a very long time. They are the vermin they are made out to be, sorry Andrew. I know we are not meant to shoot them, but I want them gone, it is that simple".

Andrew comes back at Jack.

There is now more money capturing them for zoos than there is in killing them. Why not help?

Bill finally joins in.

"They have been a menace for a long time Andrew and on this score I am inclined to agree with Jack. You live thousands of miles away in far off London. It is easy for you to be high and mighty but your livelihood is not affected by their actions, a lot of others here are"!

Andrew looks at both before answering.

"They are a timid animal and stick to the less built up areas and statistically it has been a very long time since any have been seen in some areas and what they take would be negligible".

Jack waves off Andrews comments and gets up.

"Come on". You speak a lot of rubbish Andrew".

Andrew sits where he is as Jack gets up disposing of the remainder of his cup.

"What you hear another view, so we are off again? Don't like what you hear, you get up and go again, is that it"? Andrew says rather sarcastically as he stands up.

Jack turns on him sharply.

"You are testing my patience boy. I could shoot you real easy out here and get you off my back real bloody quick?

"I have been to war too old man and have been shot at and shot others, do not test that one". Andrew warns Jack teeth clenched and raising his rifle.

"My only regret is that I do not have a bayonet with this rifle". Andrew adds threatening Jack further.

Bill gets up quickly and gets between them both.

"Now people lets not get too carried away with ourselves here, I am quite sure we will get to shoot someone else in another war sometime in the next twenty years'

Andrew and Jack stare at Bill.

"Well probably"? Bill comes back with sheepishly .

"Who"? Andrew asks.

Probably the bloody Germans again, or maybe the Japanese.  Hey we might even get to shoot at both of them". He says in a rather up beat manner.

"Not bloody likely" Jack throws back at Bill.

With that the squabble is over and the three of them head off back through the bush again, Jack out the front as usual and Bill at the rear.

#

Later in the day it has clouded over and the sky is dark, Jack looks up and turns to the other two.

"We had better go back to camp and set our traps for the night and hope we can catch one tonight".

Bill nods agreement before adding.

"They are still here in these remote forests further from settlement".

Jack nods agreement.

"There is indication of some still in the area, we'll see whether I can find them later"

At that they turn around and start to move back through the thick forest land they have come from.

## CHAPTER TWENTY THREE

The sun is low on the horizon, about to vanish for the day while the three men stand watching the trap with a possum set as bait in the trap

Jack looks up and around in the canopy and then looks at Bill and finally at Andrew with a wry grin on his face before he looks back up a tree opposite the trap.

Andrew notices, looks up the tree and then at Jack frowning, while shifting around on the spot uncomfortably.

"What are you up to you old cantankerous bastard" Andrew snarls at Jack

Bill smiles at Andrew and then looks up the tree.

Andrew notices and then looks up at the tree and steps back.

"No! No! I am not climbing up some tree like a bloody monkey or a possum (points at the possum).  I am not!  What for anyway, nothing is gained by that"?

Jack looks over at Bill and finally speaks.

"Might look dumb, but the Pommy bastard actually cottons on quick doesn't he'?

"Did rather didn't he"! comes back Bill.

"I am not climbing any bloody tree, that I give you the drum" Andrew emphasizes.

"I am not" he repeats.

"It's your Tiger not mine, I am happy to use method .303 instead of this hard yakka stuff.  It is as simple as a walk through, a single bullet properly placed and it is all over".

'What am I doing up the tree anyway"? snaps Andrew.

"Protect the trap and ensure the right animal goes into the trap". Jack tells Andrew.

"No" Andrew says and then walks off down the track still mumbling which is inaudible to the other two.

Bill looks up the tree.

"Good idea Jack, he'll do it you wait and see".

Jack nods agreement.

"He just doesn't know it yet, come on let's go and prepare him for the task". Jack tells Bill.

They both leave the trap and walk off slowly down the track as a clap of thunder goes off followed by lightning in the distance.

"Not a great night for it either" Jack adds laughing as he says it.

"Try not to show too much joy there Jack" Bill reminds him.

"Try not to Bill" Jack adds.

Andrew stands watching them momentarily silent but determined not to be going up any bloody tree, even if those two mongrels seem cock sure of it!

## CHAPTER TWENTY FOUR

Later that night, it is pitch black when the moon vanishes behind the clouds as Andrew sits propped up in the branches of a tree shivering and wet.

"Great can't see the bloody thing anyway.  Fat lot of good this is going to do" Andrew mumbles to himself.

With the moon vanishing behind the cloud cover there is a sudden clap of thunder followed by the lightning which highlights Andrew in the tree.

Andrew looks up.

"This is all I need more bloody rain, here we go again.  I am going to shoot those two old bastards when I get down from here" Andrew continues to mumble quietly to himself.

He goes to shift his position slightly and nearly loses his balance and only just avoids falling out of the tree.

"Bloody hell that was close" he says to himself.

The rain starts to come down again heavy, Andrew looks up.

"Great"!

Then he pulls the blanket around him tighter.

#

Back at the camp both Jack and Bill are asleep in there swags under the canopy while the rain comes teeming down around them.

#

Up in the tree, the rain is driving down hard still, the blanket that Andrew has wrapped around himself is soaked through while he shivers and shakes.  As quickly as it started, the rain stops and the moon peaks through briefly before the clouds close over again.

"I'll shoot that old bastard when I see him in the morning.  I am sure I would be doing this country a bloody favour" Andrew mumbles to himself.

Still mumbling to himself.

"Narrow minded old git".

#

Out in the bush the Tasmanian Tiger is watching the trap and the possum tied up in the trap.

It looks around its surroundings and then slowly, carefully it moves forward.

It stops again, looks around and then moves in closer.

There is a sudden clap of thunder and then more lightning, highlighting the trap and the scared possum tied up in the cage.

The Tasmanian Tiger vanishes into the bushes stopping after only going into the bushes a few meters it turns around and continues to watch the trap.

Within the passage of a few seconds and no other movement the Tasmanian Tiger moves in towards the trap and an easy meal.

It creeps in step after methodical step until it has a clear line of sight with the cage and then it pauses, checks its surroundings and turns its attention back to the trap and the hapless possum.

The rain starts to come down again, the Tasmanian Tiger ignoring this as it continues to concentrate on the trap and the meal that awaits it.

The Tasmanian Tiger suddenly rushes the trap, grabbing the possum by the neck, killing it instantly as the trap snaps closed behind it.

It immediately turns and rushes the entrance with the possum firmly held in its jaws, with a thud it slams into the now closed door unable to escape.

It paces up and down the trap seeking a way out with the possum held tightly in its mouth.

#

Up in the tree Andrew is watching the area where the trap is situated in the driving rain as another clap of thunder and lightning flash directly overhead and he sees something large in the trap.

He sits up instantly and stares at the trap.

"I think I have one, I think I have one" he says as he gets more excited.

Another clap of thunder and lightning goes off and Andrew sees in the trap a large shape.

He grabs his binoculars and puts them on the trap and waits for another clap of thunder and lightning, forgetting his wet miserable state in the excitement.

He waits patiently.

Nothing!

"Come on! Come on" he grumbles as he impatiently waits in excitement.

Then suddenly there is another clap of thunder followed by lightning and this time he sees it, a Tasmanian Tiger trapped in the cage.

In his excitement he nearly falls out of the tree again.

"Ah, hell that was close" he says to himself as he adjusts  and stabilizes his position perched up in the tree.

Andrew then starts to climb down the tree with the rain still coming down hard, his rifle dangling around his neck hanging down his back and his binoculars down his front.  The binoculars get in his way and he slips nearly falling.  He hangs on and with much effort he avoids falling and continues to climb down in excitement.

Before he gets to the bottom his left foot slips and he nearly falls again. He gets himself into the right position before he commences to climb down again.

On reaching the bottom of the tree he goes directly to the cage and gets a chain out of a bag he has on him and secures the cage door shut.

The Tasmanian Tiger by now is pacing up and down, the possum still in its jaws.

Andrew crouches down in front of the cage.

"Sorry about this, probably for the best Jack was only going to shoot you anyway.  See I have rescued you.  Sort of I guess".

Andrew stands up again and watches the Tasmanian Tiger in its cage.

# CHAPTER TWENTY FIVE

Bill and Jack walk slowly and wearily along the now defined path water, dripping down from the trees even though the rain has stopped.

"Any luck last night do you think"? Bill asks Jack.

"Probably not, too dark to protect the trap in reality" Jack responds with.

"It would be nice to be heading home again wouldn't it"? Bill adds.

I'd agree with that, have some of that stew the missus makes" Jack says as they come around the corner and find Andrew sitting by a fire warming up.

As the cage comes into view they spot a Tasmanian Tiger laying down in the cage not moving.

They both look at each other and then at Andrew.

Andrew finally looks up.

"Bloody soaked I am after that little exercise last night" Andrew complains.

"I can see that" Bill responds.

"Got a Thylacine there too Jack" he tells them proudly.

"Ey! That you have, that you have"! Bill adds.

You'll take that bugger back to Pommy land with you, wont you"? Jack asks with a worried tone to his voice.

"That's the plan.  Unless of course if you give me any more grief, then I will let it go out the back of your place Jack"! Andrew adds rather cheekily.

Jack sniggers and Bill laughs.

Jack glares at him as he gives a retort.

"You're the type to feel sorry for this bugger and let it go again"!

"Gone too far for that, not bloody likely Jack"! Andrew fires back at him.

Jack finally goes over to the cage and crouches down in front of it while Bill gravitates to the fire.

"Funny buggers.  Why do you just surrender like this, so passively. Where is your fight, don't you realize this is nearly the end and you lie here waiting to die, watching" Jack says quietly to the Tasmanian Tiger.

Andrew has come up behind him and watches the Tiger in the cage.

"Seen them surrender like this on many of an occasion over the years. Never have understood it.  Some animals would fight like hell in these circumstances, not the Tiger, Just ups and gives up" Jack tells Andrew."

"Now we just have to get the thing out of here", says Andrew.

"We'll put it to sleep and carry it out like we did for the one for that other Zoo many years ago" Jack responds.

"What you've done this before"? Andrew asks surprised.

In the background Bill replies.

"Twice, once for a zoo in America and one for that zoo in Hobart a few years ago".

"That's a fair walk out with a dead weight on a pole" Andrew adds.

"There is not enough of us for any other method" Jack adds.

# CHAPTER TWENTY SIX

Later that day the clouds have broken up a bit and the sun is out with a wind still blowing strongly.  Bill and Andrew are carrying the comatose Tasmanian Tiger hanging from the pole.

Jack is walking ahead of them he stops and goes over to Bill.

"My turn now Bill" Jack states.  Jack stops as he says this and waits for Bill to come up next to him.  Bill lifts the pole up and Jack moves into position and takes over the carrying of the Tiger.

"Thanks" Bill says as he releases the pole to Jack.

"You right there Andrew, do you need a rest before we carry on"? Jack asks.

""No I will be fine thanks"

They then move off, Bill flexing his muscles as they do.

"I am glad that bloody rain has stopped" Andrew complains.

"For a bloody Pom you whine a lot about the rain" Jack snaps at Andrew.

"You were not in that godforsaken tree all night either" Andrew shoots back at him.

""I am not listening to you two bitching and groaning about each other all the way back to Jacks place, shut up both of you" Bill snaps at them again as he passes them both.

They both glare at him and continue to walk in silence.

#

It is now evening and the sun is setting on the horizon, barely discernable through the forest even with the clearing of the cloud cover totally.

Andrew now walks ahead as they move along the path more carefully than they had been earlier during the day.

#

No one speaks as the Tasmanian Tiger just dangles, still in a comatose state.

It is now night and with a full moon they can see relatively well as they come around a corner.  With Jack leading again, they come out into an opening and see Jacks cottage all lit up and smoke coming out of the chimney.

"Is that a welcome sight" Jack states.

"Too bloody right it is" Bill shoots back.

"With all that walking over the last few days we did not go that far really did we"? Andrew adds surprise in his voice.

"Did not need to" Jack adds.

The three men walk out onto the flatter land picking up their pace a little as they move across the now cleared land.

Andrew walks with a smile on his face as he checks out the Tasmanian Tiger dangling in front of him.

## CHAPTER TWENTY SEVEN

Andrew walks over to Bill as the Tasmanian Tiger is now laying down in the cage on the back of the truck.

"Thanks for helping getting this project this far Bill, it is appreciated".

"That is alright, good to see you again Andrew" Bill smiles as he steps back.

Andrew steps over to Jack. "Thanks Jack, you made this possible, you really did" Andrew shakes hands with Jack as he thanks him.

"Good luck and you make sure that bloody thing ends up in that zoo in London and not in my backyard, you hear me"? Jack replies showing some paranoia.

."Don't forget to try that short cut I told you about, it will save plenty of time too" Jack fires at Andrew quickly as Andrew walks away.

Andrew then goes over and gives Jacks wife a hug and then he goes back around to the driver's side of the truck and climbs in.

He starts the truck, waves goodbye and heads off.

"That Pommy bastard is so going to let that Tiger go"!

"You are paranoid Jack. Come on I'll give you a hand catching up before you take me back into town tomorrow" Bill tells Jack

As they walk off the truck vanishes into the forest behind them.

"He will let it go" Jack continues on.

"Now Jack don't be like that" Mary says to him.

# EPILOGUE

It is coming down heavy with rain and Andrew is pouring over a map on a narrow dirt road grumbling to himself.

"Short cut my ass!  Got me stuck on some back water road, thanks Jack".

Andrew throws the map down on the seat next to him, gets out the truck and walks around the truck, checking the truck and then the cage.  As he looks away a little head pops out of a pouch and then vanishes back in. He stops in his tracks and gets closer.

"You got a joey there girl". Andrew says in surprise.

He watches her momentarily.

"Sorry old girl it does not change anything though, I need to take you to the zoo back home sorry" he says apologetically and then he goes to head back to the cab when one and then another little head bob out.

"That wont work" he shoots at the Tasmanian Tiger" and then gets in the truck.

He sits there momentarily and goes to start the truck up but hesitates.

"That was a low trick lady it really was" he mumbles to himself and then he gets out.

He climbs out onto the back of the truck and around to the front of the cage and releases the catch and opens the door to the cage.

"Go on get out before I change my mind".

He climbs out of the way behind the cage and watches.

The Tasmanian Tiger gets up and goes to the cages entrance, then looks back before it awkwardly jumps down and goes to the roads edge and stops. It looks back, Andrew waves.

"Goodbye girl, lets hope it makes a difference.

The Tasmanian Tiger is gone and Andrew watches it vanish.

"Jack is so going to kill me" Andrew says to himself and laughs as he climbs down before he gets in the cab again and starts the truck.

The End